To my mom

Henry Holt and Company, LLC
Publishers since 1866
175 Fifth Avenue
New York, New York 10010
www.henryholtchildrensbooks.com

Library of Congress Cataloging-in-Publication Data
Miller, Edward.
3 tales retold and illustrated: The three little pigs, Goldilocks and the three bears,
Three billy goats Gruff / Edward Miller.—1st ed.
p. cm.
ISBN-13: 978-0-8050-7916-6 / ISBN-10: 0-8050-7916-5
1. Tales. [1. Folklore.] I. Title. II. Title: Three tales retold and illustrated. III. Title: Three little pigs.
IV. Title: Goldilocks and the three bears. V. Title: Three billy goats gruff.
PZ8.1.M613 Tal 2007 398.2—dc22 [E] 2006043706

First Edition—2007
Printed in China on acid-free paper. ∞

1 3 5 7 9 10 8 6 4 2

The artist used the computer to create the illustrations for this book.

Visit www.edmiller.com for additional
books by Edward Miller

3

TALES RETOLD AND ILLUSTRATED

The Three Little Pigs

Goldilocks and the Three Bears

Three Billy Goats Gruff

• EDWARD MILLER •

Henry Holt and Company
New York

Fairy Tale Facts

Fairy tales are very old stories that have been told for centuries, passed down from one generation to another. Before people knew how to read and write, storytellers would spread these tales. Eventually, the stories were written down and collected in books.

The word *fairy* is used to describe tales about wonder and enchantment. Despite their name, many fairy tales do not include actual fairies. Some of the older and lesser known tales do have fairies and other magical creatures, such as elves, goblins, dragons, giants, witches, and trolls.

The Three Little Pigs and *Goldilocks and the Three Bears* are English tales collected by a Jewish writer named Joseph Jacobs (1854–1916) in 1890. He also wrote books on Jewish history.

Three Billy Goats Gruff comes from Norway. It was collected by an English writer named Sir George Dasent (1817–1896) in 1859. The troll in the story is common in Norse tales. Trolls have been depicted both as big and small, friendly and mean creatures.

Anthropomorphism is when an animal takes on human abilities, such as standing upright. Often in fairy tales, animals are shown doing human tasks and wearing clothes.

There are many versions of fairy tale classics; that's what makes the genre so interesting to read and compare.

The Three Little Pigs

Once upon a time, there were three little pigs who went looking for shelter to protect themselves from the big, bad, hungry wolf.

The first pig came across a bundle of straw. "This straw will make a fine house," said the little pig. So he built his house with straw.

The second pig came across a pile of sticks. "These sticks will make a fine house," said the little pig. So he built his house with sticks.

The third pig came across a stack of bricks. "These bricks will make a fine house," said the little pig. So he built his house with bricks.

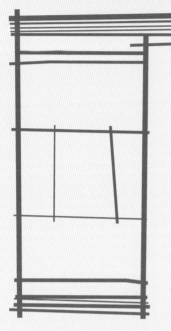

Soon after, when the first little pig was settled in his house, the big, bad wolf came knocking on his door.

"Little pig, little pig, let me in!"

"No, you will only eat me," said the pig.

"Let me in, or I'll huff, and I'll puff, and I'll *bloooooow* your house down!" said the wolf.

"No, no, not by the hair on my *chinny chin chin!*" said the pig.

So the wolf huffed, and he puffed, and he *bleeeeeew*
the straw house down and swallowed the little pig in one gulp.

Hungry for more, the wolf came knocking on the second little pig's door.

"Little pig, little pig, let me in!"

"No, you will only eat me," said the pig.

"Let me in, or I'll huff, and I'll puff, and I'll *blooooooow* your house down!" said the wolf.

"No, no, not by the hair on my *chinny chin chin!*" said the pig.

So the wolf huffed, and he puffed, and he *bleeeeeew* the stick house down and swallowed the little pig in one gulp.

Greedy for more, the wolf came knocking on the third little pig's door.

"Little pig, little pig, let me in!"

"No, you will only eat me," said the pig.

"Let me in, or I'll huff, and I'll puff, and I'll *bloooooow* your house down!" said the wolf.

NO WOLVES ALLOWED

"No, no, not by the hair on my *chinny chin chin!*" said the pig.

So the wolf huffed, and he puffed, and he huffed, and he puffed, but he couldn't blow the brick house down.

The wolf tried to outsmart the little pig by making up a lie. "Little pig, come with me to the vegetable patch, where there are turnips ready for picking. We'll make some turnip soup, and I'll be too full to eat you."

The little pig knew it was a trick because the wolf didn't like turnips. "It's too late to go tonight. Come back tomorrow at noon and we'll go together," said the pig.

The wolf agreed.

The next morning the third little
pig woke up early, ran to the field . . .

. . . picked the turnips . . .

. . . and returned safely home
before the wolf came knocking.

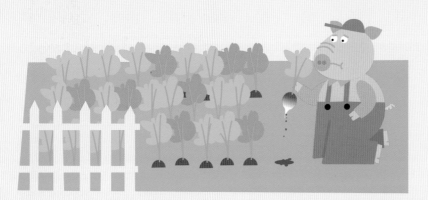

Soon the wolf appeared. "Little pig, it's time to go to the vegetable patch to pick some turnips."

"But I've already gone to the field, picked some turnips, and started the fire to make the soup," said the pig.

The wolf was angry that he'd been tricked. "Little pig, I'm going to climb down the chimney and gobble you up! *Here I come!*"

The wolf climbed onto the roof and into the chimney.
His fat belly got stuck in the narrow chute, so he burped
up the two little pigs he had swallowed and slid down.

At that moment, the third little pig lifted the top of the pot and
—*whoosh!*—the wolf fell into the boiling turnip soup. *Yowch!*

That night, the three little pigs enjoyed a tasty
turnip soup and never feared the wolf again.

Goldilocks and the Three Bears

nce upon a time, three bears lived in a cozy
house in the forest. There was a great big papa
bear, a medium-sized mama bear, and a little
baby bear.

One day the mama bear made porridge.
"This porridge is too hot to eat. Let's go for
a walk while it cools," she said.

So they did.

While they were out, a little girl
named Goldilocks wandered by. "I smell
porridge," she said. "I will ask whoever
lives here if I can have some to eat."

So Goldilocks knocked on the door,
but when nobody answered, she let
herself in.

Knock
Knock
Knock

On the table were three bowls of porridge. Goldilocks took a taste from the biggest bowl. "This porridge is too hot!" she exclaimed.

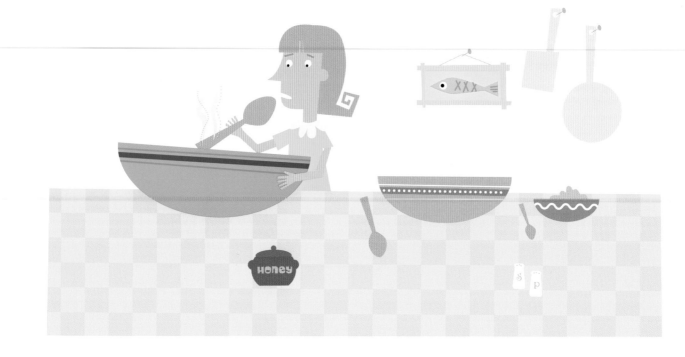

She tried the medium-sized bowl. "This porridge is too cold!" she complained.

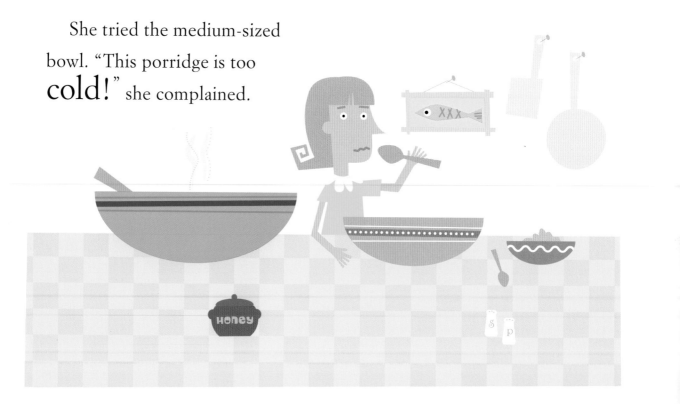

Last, she tried the little bowl. "This porridge is just right!" she said and ate it all up.

With a full tummy, Goldilocks looked for a place to rest.

In the next room were three chairs. Goldilocks sat in the biggest chair. "This chair is too hard!" she exclaimed.

She then sat in the medium-sized chair.
"This chair is too soft!" she complained.

Last, she sat in the little chair. "This chair is
just right!" she said.
But—CRACK!—the chair leg
broke under her. So she had to look for
another place to rest.

Crack!

In the bedroom were three beds. Goldilocks climbed onto the biggest bed. "This bed is too hard!" she exclaimed.

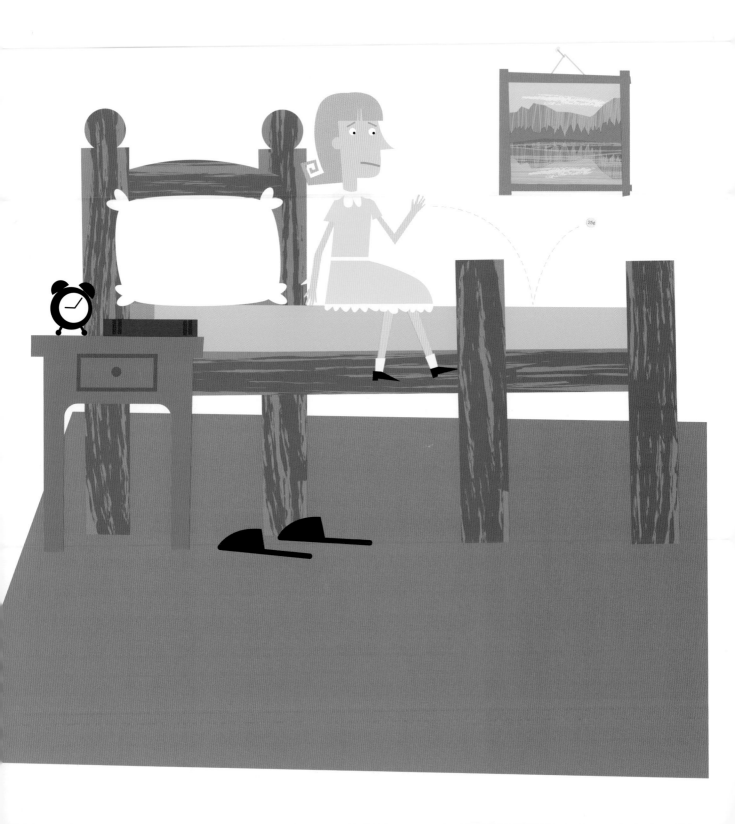

She then climbed onto the next bed. "This bed is too **soft!**"
she complained.

Last, she climbed onto the little bed. "This bed is **just right!**"
she said and fell fast asleep.

While Goldilocks dreamed pleasant dreams, the three bears came home from their walk.

"Someone's been eating my porridge!" said the papa bear.

"Someone's been eating my porridge!" said the mama bear.

"Someone's been eating my porridge and ate it all up!" cried the baby bear.

The three bears went into the next room.

"Someone's been sitting in my chair!" said the papa bear.

"Someone's been sitting in my chair!" said the mama bear.

"Someone's been sitting in my chair and broke it!" cried the baby bear.

The three bears went into the bedroom.

"Someone's been lying in my bed!" said the papa bear.

"Someone's been lying in my bed!" said the mama bear.

"Someone's been lying in my bed and lies there **still**!" cried the baby bear.

Goldilocks woke to see the three bears looking down at her.
She was very frightened.

"Don't be afraid," said the papa bear.

"You're welcome to fill your tummy and rest in our home,
but it's best to ask first," said the mama bear.

Goldilocks understood that she hadn't been very polite. So she helped the mama bear cook more porridge.

She helped the papa bear mend the chair.

And she helped the baby bear make his bed before she left for home.

After that, Goldilocks became good friends
with the three bears and visited them often.

Once upon a time, there were three billy goats named Gruff.
They wished to graze on a grassy hill on the other side of the river.
The only way across was a bridge guarded by an angry troll.

The youngest billy goat was the first to reach the bridge. *Trip, trap, trip, trap!* went the bridge as the billy goat crossed.

"Who's that trip-trapping across my bridge?" yelled the troll.

"It is I," said the billy goat. "I wish to graze on the grassy hill on the other side of this bridge."

"Oh, no you don't!" said the troll. "I'm going to eat you up!"

The billy goat thought quickly, "Why would you want to eat me? I'm the smallest billy goat. Wait for my older brother to cross. He is much bigger than I am."

"All right," said the troll. "I'll eat you when you return from grazing."

Trip
Trap

Trip
Trap

Next came the second billy goat Gruff. *Trip, trap, trip, trap!* went the bridge as he crossed.

"Who's that trip-trapping across my bridge?" yelled the troll.

"It is I," said the second billy goat. "I wish to graze on the grassy hill on the other side of this bridge."

"Oh, no you don't!" said the troll. "I'm going to eat you up!"

The billy goat thought quickly, "Why would you want to eat me? Wait for my older brother to cross. He is much bigger than I am."

"All right," said the troll. "I'll eat you when you return from grazing."

Trip
Trap

Trip
Trap

Trip
Trap

Trip
Trap

Last came the third billy goat Gruff. *Trip, trap, trip, trap!* went the bridge as he crossed.

"Who's that trip-trapping across my bridge?" yelled the troll.

"It is I," said the third billy goat. "I wish to graze on the grassy hill on the other side of this bridge with my brothers."

"Oh, no you don't!" said the troll. "I'm going to eat you up!"

With all his might, the billy goat **charged** at
the angry troll and **butted** him with his horns.

The troll fell off the bridge and tumbled into the river below.

The third billy goat Gruff crossed the bridge and joined his brothers on the hill for a fine lunch of grass and flowers. And they were never bothered by the troll again.